LUCKY LAZLO

For Christine,
my lucky charm and the love of my life

First published in Great Britain 2017 by Walker Books Ltd
87 Vauxhall Walk, London SE11 5HJ

This edition published 2018

2 4 6 8 10 9 7 5 3 1

© 2016 Steve Light

The right of Steve Light to be identified as author and illustrator of this work has been asserted
by him in accordance with the Copyright, Designs and Patents Act 1988

This book has been typeset in Stempel Schneidler

Printed in China

British Library Cataloguing in Publication Data:
a catalogue record for this book is available from the British Library

ISBN 978-1-4063-7830-6

www.walker.co.uk

LUCKY LAZLO

Steve Light

WALKER BOOKS
AND SUBSIDIARIES

LONDON • BOSTON • SYDNEY • AUCKLAND

Lazlo was in love.

He bought a rose from
the flower-seller.

The last red one –
how lucky!

The girl he loved was starring in a play.

Lucky Lazlo had a ticket – a front-row seat
for *Alice in Wonderland* at the Peacock Theatre.

Then Lazlo
ran into a bit
of bad luck.

Ouch!

And the chase was on…

The cat dashed right past everyone getting ready for the performance.

He got tangled in the tailor's thread.

He tried to hide in a tuba!

BRUM PA PA

FRIDAY
NOV.
23

He explored the prop table.

SMASH!

He scampered through the orchestra as the music began.
"MIAOW!"

He didn't stop for tea.

No room! No room!

He did stop to gaze at something handsome in the mirror.

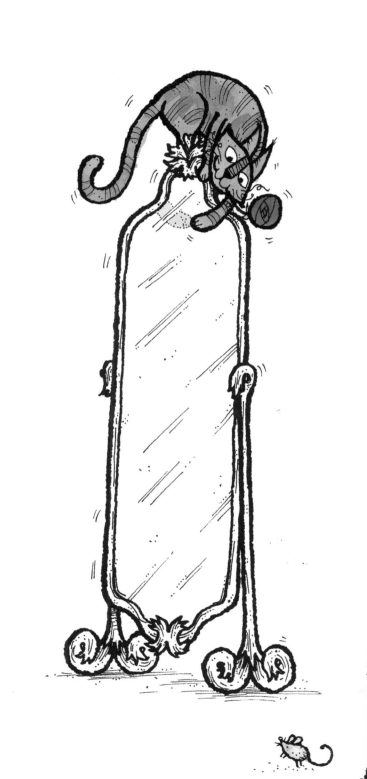
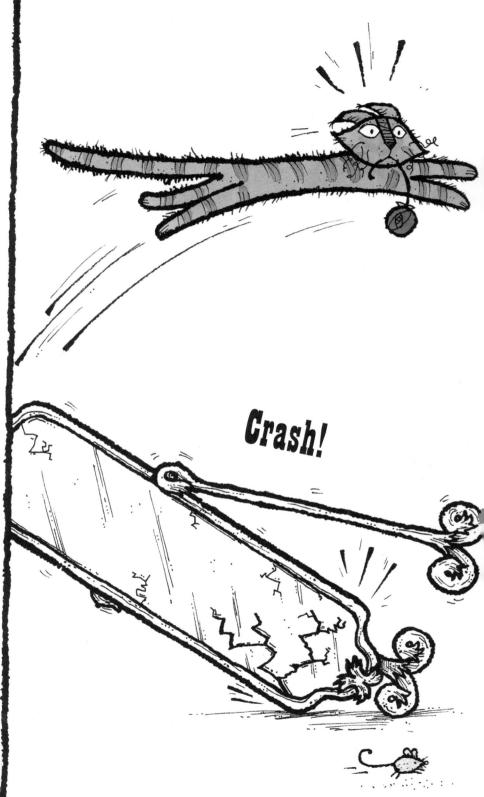

Crash!

The cat had something
new to play with.
Lazlo was in luck!

(Not everyone was.)

He was on a roll!

Whoa!

Uh-oh!

Aha!

He stole the show!

Bravo, **BRAVO!**

Lucky ♥ Lazlo!

Author's Note

What started as a simple love story set in a theatre became a madcap adventure involving superstitions. The more research I did, the more I was drawn to the superstitions and harbingers of good and bad luck surrounding theatres and actors. It's no wonder that things go wrong for Lazlo and the cast and crew at the Peacock Theatre. They have broken every superstitious rule in the book! See how many you can spot. Good luck … er – *Break a leg!*

Some Theatrical Superstitions

The presence of peacock feathers in a theatre is said to bring bad luck. The superstition derives from the notion that the peacock feather contains the evil eye, which will bring disaster.

Flowers should never be presented before a performance.

Cats are considered both good and bad luck. The cat in this story brings a little of both. It's lucky to have a cat in the theatre – but bad luck if it runs across the stage during a performance.

Applying make-up with a rabbit's foot is meant to ensure good luck. Apparently, no one remembered to do that!

Shoes or hats on a table in a dressing room bring bad luck, and real money should never be used onstage for the same reason.

It is bad luck to exit a dressing room right foot first. Actors make sure to step out left foot first.

Shakespeare's *Macbeth* should never be referred to by name – "the Scottish play" is preferred.

It is bad luck to open a show on a Friday.

November 23 holds a special place in theatre lore. On that estimated date in 534 BCE, a Greek poet named Thespis became the first person to speak lines as an individual actor onstage – hence the term "thespian".

In the orchestra, good luck follows when instruments don't need to be tuned before a show. All the instruments at the Peacock Theatre need to be tuned on this night!

No theatre should ever be "dark", even when unoccupied. There should always be a ghost light. There are a few theories about this superstition. Some believe the light is meant to ward off ghosts; others believe its presence gives ghosts enough illumination to act in their own plays, thereby keeping them out of other mischief. More practically, the ghost light prevents people crossing the stage from falling off in the darkness – possibly becoming ghosts themselves.

Whistling in the theatre is said to bring bad luck. Years ago, sailors were hired to do the rigging. They used specific whistle tones to communicate with one another, so whistling by anyone else could cause confusion and result in dropped sets – a very dangerous situation.

Never say "good luck" to an actor. "Break a leg" is preferred. One theory about this refers to audiences in ancient Greece, who stomped their feet instead of clapping. Reacting to a strong performance could cause an audience member to "break a leg". Much later, in vaudeville, only actors who were called onstage got paid, so breaking a leg – referring to the post separating the stage from backstage – meant the actor would be paid for that evening's work. Still another explanation refers to an actor bowing at the end of the show, thereby bending, or "breaking", a leg.

Three candles onstage is a no-no. It is said that the person nearest the shortest candle will be the next to marry – or the next to die.

Knitting in the wings can bring bad luck, not only because the needles can easily fall and cause someone to trip, but also because it was once common for fights to break out in theatres, and knitting needles made handy weapons.

Mirrors should never appear onstage. Broken mirrors are considered bad luck nearly everywhere – the theatre is no exception.

A kiss from a loved one is always considered lucky – in any location.